To,
George +
Olivia,
Ho

Zoom to the Moon

Written & illustrated by Inderjit Puaar

In loving memory of Grandpa

"Grandpa,"
said Bradley,
"can I fly to
the moon?"

Grandpa smiled,
"With your magic
puzzle you can zoom!"

So off Bradley went. He flew deep into space, he flew higher and higher, "Oh what a dark place!"

After a long time, Bradley was finally there,

he looked back at Earth, but he had no fear.

He spotted four little aliens with tiny green ears,

"Aarrgghh!" they screamed and ran away in tears.

"Don't be scared. I am only a big red bus!"
Bradley wondered why they made such a fuss.
Bradley explained, "I'm similar to a spaceship.
I drive humans around when they fancy a trip."

The alien smiled, his eyes shone brightly as the sun.

His new alien friends looked like so much fun!

One alien said kindly, "You can stay with us.

We have never made friends with a big red bus."

Everybody thought Bradley was very cool. The aliens said, "Hurry up! Let's go to school."

Bradley sang, "Mercury, Venus, Earth and Mars, Jupiter, Saturn, Uranus, Neptune plus stars."

His friend Astro invited Bradley to his home,
the alien house had a big shiny glass dome.
Bradley met Astro's mum, dad and sister Sky,
he told them how his puzzle allowed him to fly.

At dinner time, everyone got ready to eat,

they gave Bradley food that looked like a treat.

The alien food was bright red, orange and blue,

"BEEP BEEP! This food is so yummy, thank you!"

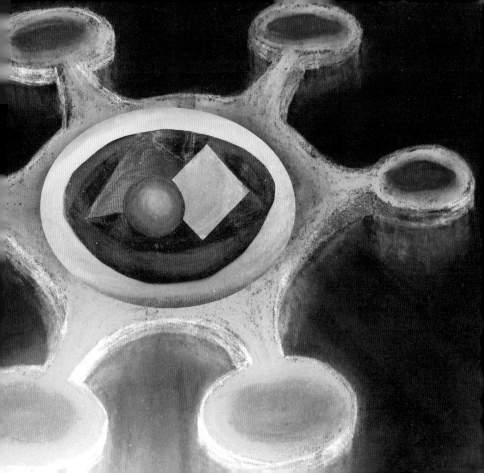

Bradley went exploring with his new friend,

then he showed him his puzzle piece at the end.

"What do you think this sign here could mean?"

"It means strength," said Astro, who was just as keen.

"**BEEP BEEP!** Super strong powers!" Bradley was happy,
Astro suddenly shouted, "Move quick! Make it snappy."

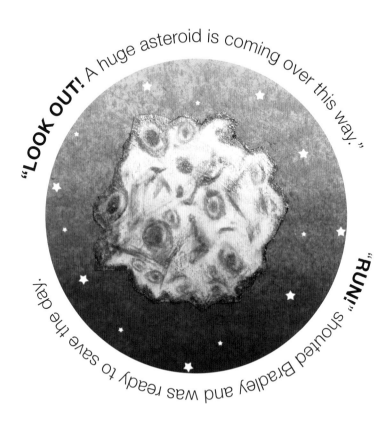

"LOOK OUT! A huge asteroid is coming over this way."

"RUN!" shouted Bradley and was ready to save the day.

Bradley said, "I must believe I have power and am strong!"

BOOM! He smashed the asteroid into dust before long.

"Hip hip hooray! Bradley the Bus, you saved us all."

Everyone threw him a party in a great big hall.

"Bradley, you were so brave!" Bradley felt so proud.

"BEEP BEEP!" he hooted and made sure it was loud.

Everyone celebrated and had a great time,

Bradley was given a medal with a lovely shine.

Bradley missed Grandpa, he wanted to go back.

He thanked everybody and began to pack.

Bradley sadly said goodbye to Astro his mate,

Grandpa was waiting. He didn't want to be late.

"Fancy a ride in our spaceship?" asked Astro's dad.

"BEEP BEEP! Yes please!" said Bradley but then felt sad.

"I'm going to miss you all, make sure you visit me."

"Of course we will!" they replied. "Just wait and see."

The spaceship landed near Big Ben during the day.

"Goodbye!" said Astro. "We hope you enjoyed your stay!"

"Bye!" said Bradley. The spaceship whizzed off into space,
Grandpa was happy to see Bradley back in his place.

Bradley told Grandpa about his time on the moon,
he told him about the superpower he would use soon.
Bradley looked at his puzzle and said, **"BEEP BEEP!"**